Chapter 1

THE DARK SHADOW

The theatre at Harrison Ford High School
was empty. It was silent and full of shadows.
The only light came from a single dim bulb,
hanging above the stage.

The director and the actors had all
gone home. No one would be back until
the rehearsal the next night.

From a dark corner of the stage, a person
stepped forward. The dark shadow with spiky
hair moved quickly backstage to the area
directly behind the set.

The figure made a strange movement. Carefully, it touched the back of one of the fake walls. It seemed to be hiding something. Something no one else would see. Something invisible to the naked eye.

Then, smoothly, silently, the figure slipped away.

CURTAINS!

A HIGH SCHOOL MUSICAL MYSTERY

by Michael Dahl
illustrated by Tiffany Prothero

Librarian Reviewer
Marci Peschke

Reading Consultant
Elizabeth Stedem

www.raintreepublishers.co.uk
Visit our website to find out
more information about
Raintree books.

To order:
☎ Phone 0845 6044371
🖶 Fax +44 (0) 1865 312263
🖳 Email myorders@capstonepub.co.uk

Customers from outside the UK please telephone +44 1865 312262

Raintree is an imprint of Capstone Global Library Limited,
a company incorporated in England and Wales having its registered
office at 7 Pilgrim Street, London, EC4V 6LB
– Registered company number: 6695582

"Raintree" is a registered trademark of Pearson Education Limited,
under licence to Capstone Global Library Limited

Text © Stone Arch Books, 2009
First published in United Kingdom by Capstone Global Library in 2010
The moral rights of the proprietor have been asserted.

Edited in the UK by Laura Knowles
Art Director: Heather Kindseth
Graphic Designer: Kay Frase
Originated by Capstone Global Ltd
Printed and bound in China by CTPS

Photo Credits
Shutterstock/R. Gino Santa Maria, cover, 1

ISBN 978 1 406215 78 6 (hardback)
14 13 12 11 10
10 9 8 7 6 5 4 3 2 1

ISBN 978 1 406215 94 6 (paperback)
14 13 12 11 10
10 9 8 7 6 5 4 3 2 1

British Library Cataloguing in Publication Data
Dahl, Michael.
Curtains. -- (School mysteries)
813.5'4-dc22
A full catalogue record for this book is
available from the British Library.

CONTENTS

SMASH HIT

Kyle Sutton ran down the hall to his locker. He grabbed his script from the top shelf and banged the locker door shut. Then he raced back down the hall, heading towards the school theatre.

The hallway that led to the theater auditorium was full of glass and steel beams and sunlight. As soon as he opened the theatre's double doors, Kyle stepped into a world of shadows.

A single spotlight shone on a person standing on the stage. It was the drama teacher and the musical's director, J.B. She was talking to the cast and crew of the play. They were seated in the auditorium, facing her.

"Thank you for joining us, Kyle," J.B. said. Everyone's eyes turned to watch as Kyle entered.

J.B.'s full name was Joyce Boxer, but she preferred to be called by her initials. She was tall and muscular, had short blonde hair, and was not a person to mess with. She had a stare that could drill through a steel wall. Her voice could carry to the top row of the auditorium without the help of a microphone.

"As soon as Amber gets here, we will begin," J.B. continued. "I don't want to have to repeat myself. Remember, people, theatre is a commitment. If you can't be at rehearsals on time, then don't bother coming at all."

Brendan Foster, a tall, blonde boy sitting in the front row, gave a snort.

J.B. looked at him sharply. "I hope you're not getting a cold," she said. "That wouldn't be good for the star of the show, would it?"

"No, J.B.," said Brendan. He sat up straighter in his seat.

"Kyle, over here," whispered a girl's voice. It was Megan Oliver. She was the play's stage manager. She was also Kyle's only friend at Harrison Ford High School.

Kyle quietly slipped into the seat next to Megan. She had a paperback book in her hand, like always. "What are you reading now?" he whispered.

"It's Agatha Christie," said Megan. "You know, the Queen of Crime?"

Kyle shook his head. "Never heard of her," he said.

"Are you serious?" said Megan. "How can you grow up as a normal person and not know who Agatha Christie is?"

"I'm not normal," said Kyle, grinning.

"Who is, at this school?" asked Megan.

"Do you mind?" came another voice.

Kyle leaned forward in his seat and glanced past Megan. The voice had come from Martian. The spiky-haired guy's real name was Martin, but he preferred his nickname. Martian had written the play they were working on.

"I'm trying to think," said Martian. He frowned and stared at the screen of a small laptop. He tapped on the keys while he chewed his lip angrily.

Kyle leaned over and whispered to Megan, "I thought Martian had finished writing the script."

Megan rolled her eyes. Her dark curls swung as she shook her head. "The genius is finished writing the play," she said. "But he's keeping track of all the mistakes that the actors make."

"Mistakes?" said Kyle.

"You know how Brendan likes to make up lines and jokes during rehearsals?" said Megan. "Well, Martian types them all down. If you change one word in a line, he remembers it. Then he prints out a note for each actor who changed his words. He acts like his little play is some incredible masterpiece."

"Well, the play is sort of cool," Kyle said.

"It's not Shakespeare," said Megan.

The play, called *Starcups!*, was a musical play. Martian wrote the words. Harrison Ford High School band and orchestra students had written the songs.

The story took place at an imaginary coffee shop, where people liked to hang out with their friends.

Brendan played the guy behind the counter. Amber Long played the lonely girl who visited him every day after school.

Kyle played Brendan's best friend, the class clown, who was always getting into trouble. There were about fifteen other kids in the cast. They played students, employees, and customers. A small trio – electric guitar, drums, and keyboard – provided the music.

Everyone waited quietly in the theatre. Finally, the doors to the auditorium opened and Amber Long walked in.

"Sorry, everyone," Amber called out. She loudly stomped over to an empty seat.

"Finally," said J.B. "Now if I can have everyone's attention–"

Just then, Kyle heard a strange moan from the dark space above the stage. "Look out!" yelled Brendan. He jumped onto the stage and tackled J.B. with the force of a rugby player.

As Brendan and the director tumbled onto the floor, a heavy light fell from the ceiling. It landed right where J.B. had been standing.

Chapter 3

LEADING ROLE

For several moments the theatre was deadly silent. Then everyone began to speak at once.

"Are you all right, J.B.?" asked Amber.

"That was amazing!" said Megan.

"This will look great on my blog," said Martian. He pulled out his mobile phone and snapped a few shots of the broken light.

"Good move, Brendan," said Kyle. "That's what I call light on your feet."

Megan looked at Kyle and rolled her eyes. "Very funny," she said.

J.B. slowly stood up. She ran a hand through her short blond hair.

"I can't believe that just happened," said Amber.

Everyone stared at the fallen light. It had made an ugly dent in the wooden floor. Broken glass littered the stage.

"I don't know how that could have happened," J.B. said. "Megan, get one of the tech guys to take a look up there before we leave tonight. I don't want another accident to happen."

"Got it, J.B.," said Megan.

"That's right where I stand during my big song," said Amber. She shivered. "Can you imagine what would have happened if the light had fallen then?"

"Yeah," said Kyle. "The song would have sounded better."

Everyone laughed.

"Let's get this mess cleaned up, and start with Act Two," said J.B. She fixed her ice-blue eyes on Kyle and pointed at him. "Kyle, come with me," she ordered.

Kyle felt a chill go down his spine. He was convinced that he had lost the power to move, but somehow, he was able to follow the director. J.B. led him to a corner of the stage. She picked up her shoulder bag, which had been sitting on the floor.

"Kyle," she said. "Can you keep a secret?"

Kyle nodded.

"I'm already working on the next play, the one we'll be doing in the spring," J.B. said. "And I think you'd be good for it."

"Thanks, J.B.," said Kyle.

"I'm not complimenting you," J.B. said. "I'm stating a fact. You're a smart young man. And talented." J.B. reached into her bag and pulled out a script. She handed it to Kyle.

"I want you to read that for me," she said.

"Right now?" asked Kyle.

J.B. almost smiled. "You've got a lot of potential, Kyle, but not a lot of experience. This is your first play, isn't it?" she asked.

Kyle nodded. "I thought it would be a good way to meet people," he said. "I've only been at Harrison a few months."

"You didn't try out for plays at your other school?" asked J.B.

"No," said Kyle. "I was on the football team." J.B. gave him a funny look. "It was a small school," he explained.

"When I asked you to read that script for me, I meant try out," J.B. explained. "In other words, audition. I want you to look over the script and try out for the lead part."

Kyle couldn't believe his ears. The lead?

"It's a great part," J.B. added. "Only two people at this school could do it. You and Brendan. Read it over and be ready to try out for me and Megan in a few days."

"Cool," said Kyle. "Thanks."

J.B. walked briskly back to the centre of the stage. A boy with a broom and dustpan was sweeping up the broken glass.

Megan was sitting in the second row of the auditorium, her script open on her knees. She was waiting for the actors in Act Two to take their places when the stage was clean.

Kyle jogged over to her. "Look at this," he said, waving the script at her.

Megan smiled. "I know," she said. "J.B. told me yesterday. Then she swore me to secrecy on my goldfish's grave."

Kyle sat down and looked at the script. *City Lights: The Young Charlie Chaplin.* "Wow!" said Kyle. "Charlie Chaplin was a comedy genius. J.B. wants me to try out for this?"

"Charlie Chaplin was one of the biggest names in movies," said Megan. "He practically created film comedy. Did you ever see that movie about him? You should rent it."

Kyle couldn't believe his luck. He had tried out for *Starcups!* almost as a joke to himself. He thought it would be fun to meet people and make friends.

Then, once rehearsals started, he found out how much he actually enjoyed acting. He liked working with a team to put together a show.

Whenever the cast or Megan laughed at his lines during a practice, he felt satisfied. More satisfied than he'd ever felt on the football field.

"So, who do you think has the best chance of getting the part?" Kyle asked Megan.

Megan smiled. "You, of course."

"You have to say that," said Kyle. "You're my friend."

"I don't have to say anything," said Megan. "Besides, who says I'm your friend?"

Just then, Kyle glanced up at the stage. People were getting ready to start Act Two. Brendan was standing up there, motionless, while people moved around him. The taller boy stood with his arms folded, a frown on his face. Brendan's gaze was on the script in Kyle's hands.

Brendan did not look happy.

------ Chapter 4 ------

FALLING WALL

The next day after school, Kyle was the first person at rehearsal. He chucked his rucksack and jacket on to an empty seat. He pulled the Charlie Chaplin script from his back pocket. Then he jumped up on to the stage, sat down, crossed his legs, and read over his lines.

"It would be amazing to play Charlie Chaplin," thought Kyle. But he knew it wouldn't happen. J.B. had said that only he or Brendan had the talent to play the part, and Brendan had a lot more acting experience.

Kyle remembered the look that Brendan had given him the night before. Brendan really wanted that part. His look said that he would do anything to get it.

As Kyle quietly read the script, a soft sound caught his attention. It seemed to come from a back corner of the auditorium. Was it a mouse? Or maybe he wasn't the first one inside the theatre after all.

"Hey, is someone there?" Kyle called.

"It's only me," came a voice. Kyle turned around and saw Martian sitting near the back of the auditorium, typing away on his laptop.

"Are you always working on that thing?" asked Kyle.

"This thing happens to be my life," said Martian without looking up. "My computer has become part of my body. Without it, I would die."

"Ah," said Kyle. He stretched his legs out in front of him. Then he pulled off his hat and scratched his head. "So, did you get some good photos for your blog yesterday?" he asked.

Martian shrugged. "I already put them online. You'll have to look when you get the chance," he said.

Kyle stared down at the dent in the wooden stage floor. It was hard to believe that the heavy stage light had fallen only yesterday. J.B. was lucky she hadn't been hit.

"That could have killed J.B., don't you think?" said Kyle.

"I guess," said Martian. "By the way, I made some notes for you about rehearsal yesterday. First, yesterday you said, 'I have a report due for class tomorrow.' The line is actually, 'Tomorrow, I have a report due for class.' "

"Uh, sorry," said Kyle.

"Sorry for what?" asked Megan, entering the room. She was followed by a few other actors and crew members.

"I was just going over some lines with Martian," replied Kyle.

"That's right," said Megan, rolling her eyes. "It has to be perfect."

"Yes, it does!" Martian exclaimed.

"What are you doing sitting in the dark, Martian?" asked Megan. "You'll go blind working like that."

"Great, then I'll go blind," said Martian. "I'll still be able to hear every wrong word."

Megan shook her head. As she walked towards the front of the stage, she passed Kyle and said, "Cool hair. I never noticed it being spiky before."

"It's not me," said Kyle. "My hat messes it all up."

"I meant Martian," said Megan. "But your hair is just as cool." She laughed. "Actors!" she said. "They think everything's about them!"

The next hour and a half went smoothly. The cast rehearsed Act One. Martian typed on his laptop.

"We'll start adding songs next week," J.B. said. "The musicians will join our rehearsals then. Everyone must memorize their lines."

There were a few groans from the cast. "No excuses," said J.B. "And Amber? When you say your lines, you're not cheering at a football game. I appreciate that you're loud enough for everyone in the auditorium to hear you, but not every line has to be shouted."

Amber looked down at her feet. "Yes, J.B.," she said quietly.

J.B. looked over at Brendan, who was standing behind the fake Starcups coffee shop counter. His hand was raised.

"I have a question," Brendan said. "When Kyle and I are talking in that first scene, does he have to make those goofy faces?"

"What's wrong with my face?" asked Kyle.

"Everyone's going to be watching your face and not listening to what I say," said Brendan.

"What's wrong with that?" asked Kyle.

Suddenly, Amber screamed. Martian yelled.

Part of the set was leaning forward at a dangerous angle. The walls of the set were built in separate sections. Each wall section was about ten feet tall and six feet wide. One of the wall sections, the one right behind Brendan, was falling straight towards the star of the show.

Chapter 5

MARTIAN'S IDEA

Brendan spun around and saw the wall section falling towards him. He quickly ducked down behind the coffee counter.

Whack! The wall section slammed into the counter. It bounced and wobbled, then was still.

Luckily, the wall section had hit the counter instead of hitting Brendan. He had been able to squeeze into the small space between the wall section, the counter, and the floor.

"I'm okay," called Brendan.

Brendan crawled out on to the open stage floor. Kyle helped him to his feet.

Brendan frowned at Kyle. "What? You don't have a joke this time, funny guy?" Brendan asked.

"People, this should not be happening," said J.B. "We're getting sloppy. Sloppy about hanging lights, sloppy about building sets, and sloppy with our lines. Everyone needs to stay focused. Do your jobs, and do them right. Megan, come with me."

Megan quickly grabbed her script and notes and walked towards J.B. Before the two of them left the stage, J.B. turned and faced the cast. "Rehearsal's over," she said. "But I want everyone to go home and learn their lines!"

Kyle and Brendan helped push the wall section back into place.

A few of the crew members found iron weights to hold the wall's feet in place. Another kid started nailing the wall section to the one next to it.

Kyle gathered up his jacket, script, and rucksack. As he headed towards the theatre doors, he saw Martian waiting for him.

"That's the second time," Martian said, nodding towards the stage.

"The second accident, you mean?" said Kyle.

"Those weren't accidents," said Martian. "Someone is doing this on purpose."

"On purpose? You watch too much TV," said Kyle.

"I never watch TV," said Martian. "Someone wants to shut down my play. By the way, do you have any comments about this that I can put on my blog?"

"Yeah, just one comment. Who would want to shut down *Starcups!*?" asked Kyle.

Martian gave Kyle a strange look. "Don't you have a few ideas?" he asked. "You're a smart young man." Then Martian took off down the hall.

"Smart young man"? That's what J.B. had called Kyle the other night, before she handed him the Charlie Chaplin script. "Is Martian spying on me?" Kyle wondered. "That kid creeps me out. Even if he is a genius."

Kyle sat in the corridor outside the theatre's double doors. He didn't want to go home until he talked to Megan.

Half an hour later, she finally pushed through the doors. Her arms were full of books, scripts, and papers. She jumped when she saw Kyle. "Oh, you scared me," said Megan. "I didn't know anyone was there."

"Sorry," said Kyle. "I just wanted to –"

"Make sure I got home safely?" said Megan.

"Uh, yeah. And I wanted to ask you a question," Kyle told her. "About those accidents."

"Yeah," said Megan. "It's like we're under a curse or something."

"Or something," said Kyle. "You think they're accidents?"

Megan stopped and stared. "I don't think it's a ghost, if that's what you mean," she said.

"Martian thinks someone is causing those accidents on purpose," said Kyle.

"Martian is from another planet," said Megan.

Kyle gave a sigh of relief. "So, you do think they're just accidents," he said.

"Not so fast," said Megan. "I don't know, yet. I might have to consult Agatha Christie about that."

"The Queen of Crime?" Kyle asked.

Megan smiled. She said, "That's right." She winked and added, "You're a smart young man."

"Don't say that," said Kyle.

Megan shrugged. "Whatever," she said. "Well, in Agatha Christie's mysteries, accidents happened to people. But the accidents turned out to be the work of someone else."

"But who?" asked Kyle, confused. "Who would want to shut down the show?"

"Does Martian think somebody wants to shut down the show?" asked Megan. "He is so worried about his show not being perfect. He just doesn't get it. Plays get put on because dozens of people work together."

"Right," Kyle said.

Megan went on, "Everyone gets to add his or her part. It's not the work of just one person. Oof! He makes me so mad sometimes."

"Oof? You actually said oof?" said Kyle, grinning.

"Pretend you didn't hear that," said Megan. "Come on. Let's go to a real coffee shop and talk about this. Hopefully, no walls will fall over on us."

Chapter 6

AMBER'S EXIT

Café Ole was a coffee shop a few streets away from the school. On the front window, it had a painting of a bull and a bullfighter. Inside, an iPod system played Spanish pop music. When Megan and Kyle got there, several other people from the musical were already inside. The smells of coffee, milk, hot chocolate, and cookies filled the air.

Two guys from the stage crew, Will and Jake, waved Megan and Kyle over to their table.

"Hi, guys," said Will. He had scruffy hair and dark glasses. Jake was wearing a motorcycle T-shirt and an earring.

"What a crazy night," Kyle said.

"I know that wall section was safe," said Will. "I worked on it myself."

Jake nodded. "We don't want J.B. blaming us," he said. "We put weights on all the wall sections. None of them should be able to move."

"So someone had to take off the weights for that wall to fall over?" asked Kyle.

"They wouldn't walk off by themselves," explained Jake.

"Who would do something like that?" asked Megan.

"Don't look at me," said Will. "All I know is, when we checked the wall section after it fell over, Jake and I saw that the weights had been moved. They were a few feet away."

Kyle was about to say something when he heard shouting at the other end of the coffee shop. A guy wearing a Harrison Ford High School black and gold letter jacket was standing over the table where Brendan and Amber were sitting. He was loud and angry.

"Who's he?" Kyle asked. The guy in the jacket had hair that was shaved off on the sides, and short on top.

"And what's up with his '80s hair?" Jake asked.

"That's Rick Thomas," said Megan. "Amber's boyfriend. He's on the wrestling team."

Brendan stood up and faced Rick. Both of their faces were red. Brendan was a lot taller than Rick, but Rick was built like a tank. Kyle thought Rick's jacket must have been specially made to handle all the extra muscles.

"Things are going to get ugly," said Jake, sipping his coffee.

Rick turned away from Brendan. "Come on, Amber. Let's get out of here," he said.

Amber looked embarrassed, but she gathered up her things and said goodbye to her friends. Brendan remained standing.

As Amber hurried out of the coffee shop, everyone could hear Rick's angry voice. "You shouldn't be in that play anymore. It's too dangerous," he said.

Megan looked at Kyle. "Yikes," she said.

"How would her boyfriend already know about the wall falling over?" asked Kyle.

"Everybody has a mobile phone," Megan pointed out. "And if you want to make a public announcement, just tell Amber. She can text ten people in ten seconds. I think she has two extra thumbs."

Kyle thought about Martian taking photos with his mobile phone. He wondered if pictures of that night's accident were already on the writer's blog.

"Rick might have a point," Megan continued. "So far, no one has been hurt by these accidents. But if they keep happening, it's only a matter of time."

"Maybe we should consult your friend Agatha Christie," said Kyle.

Chapter 7

MAKING THE CUT

The next day, at lunchtime, Kyle and Megan sat at a table in a far corner of the school library.

Megan had set out sheets of paper arranged in piles. Everyone connected to the musical had his or her name written on a separate sheet of paper.

"What's all this?" asked Kyle.

"These are all the suspects," said Megan.

"What do you mean?" Kyle asked.

"This is what the detectives in Agatha Christie's books do," Megan explained. "They make a list of everyone they think is guilty. They examine their motives, and write down where everyone was during the accidents."

"There are a lot of people working on *Starcups!*," Kyle pointed out.

"Some of them aren't suspects," said Megan. "The musicians haven't even been in the theatre yet. I think we can ignore any of the new people. They don't know their way around the auditorium."

"Why does that matter?" asked Kyle.

Megan explained, "If you don't know your way around the auditorium, you won't know how to get up to the light system. There's a whole set of walkways and metal stairs up there in the dark. Only someone who knows his way around –"

"Or her way around," added Kyle.

"True. Or her way around," agreed Megan. "All I'm saying is that only someone who's done plays here before would know how to get to the lights hanging over the stage."

"A new person could do it," said Kyle.

"Not likely," said Megan.

"A smart new person like me could," Kyle said.

"You're different," said Megan.

"Am I a suspect?" asked Kyle hopefully.

"Let's look at my list," said Megan. She handed Kyle a sheet of paper. On the top, Megan had written, "Main Suspects." There was a list of names.

Brendan F

Amber L

Rick T

Martian P

JB

Megan O

Kyle S

"Wow! I am a suspect!" said Kyle.

"I had to put you in," said Megan. "You've always been around whenever an accident took place."

"But you put your own name down, too," Kyle said.

Megan shrugged. "I'm the stage manager," she explained. "I know where everything is. It wouldn't be fair if I left myself out."

"Well, are you the criminal?" asked Kyle.

"How could you even think that?" asked Megan.

"You didn't answer the question," Kyle said.

"Look at the list," said Megan.

"What about the tech guys, and the other cast members? Why did you leave them off?" asked Kyle.

"Criminals are usually people who have something important at stake," Megan explained. "This list shows the people who have the most to gain or lose if the show is a success, or a failure. These are the people that the play is most important to."

"Hmmm, I guess so," Kyle said. He stared at the list. "So Rick Thomas is a suspect, since he wants Amber out of the show?"

Megan nodded. "If the show is cancelled, he gets to spend more time with Amber," she said. "Plus, then Amber's life is free from more danger."

"And Martian wants the show stopped because he thinks everyone is ruining it?" asked Kyle.

"Right again," said Megan. "Martian is such a perfectionist. He would rather we close the show than make any mistakes."

"What about Brendan?" Kyle asked. "Why is he a suspect? He doesn't want the show to close."

"No, I think he wants the show to succeed," said Megan. "He's the star, after all. Maybe he planned those accidents to make himself look more important. He did save J.B. from the falling light. That made him a hero."

"Yeah, but he's not acting like the big hero," said Kyle. "And he already has the lead."

Megan frowned. "Yeah, you're right," she said quietly.

"And why would Amber do it?" asked Kyle.

"So she can get out of the play without quitting," said Megan. "She has a reputation for being such a go-getter. She hates to look like a quitter."

"So she bashes in J.B.'s head so she can spend more time with the Hulk?" Kyle asked, shaking his head. "I really don't think so. That doesn't make sense."

Megan began gathering up all her papers. "Well, there's another thing Agatha Christie says about criminals," she said.

"What's that?" asked Kyle.

"The guilty person is usually the person you suspect the least," Megan said.

Kyle thought a moment. "That would make it you," he said with a grin.

"Or you," said Megan seriously.

Kyle nodded. "Yes, I do have an evil mind sometimes," he said. "Perhaps I'm causing these accidents to get Brendan out of the way. Then I will step in, take his part, save the show, and get all the glory!"

"Now you're creeping me out," Megan said.

"I'm the new kid at school," Kyle went on. "No one really knows me. I'm the unknown. X. That's me. My secret identity. X the Unknown."

"Stop it, Kyle," said Megan.

"Want to know how I did it?" Kyle asked. "I have help, a partner in crime. It's one of the tech guys. Jake. Or maybe Will. I paid them to loosen the bolts on the light. And I had them push the wall over when no one was looking."

"I don't like it when you talk like that," said Megan. "I have to get to my next lesson."

"I thought you were supposed to meet with J.B. about the costumes," Kyle said.

"After school," said Megan. Then she slipped her bag over her shoulder and sailed out of the library.

"Maybe I shouldn't have said all that," Kyle thought. "Maybe I'm a better actor than I realized."

He left the library and walked down the corridor to his next lesson. As he passed the corridor that led to the theatre, he saw Megan stepping inside. "I thought she had to hurry to class," Kyle thought.

He still had ten minutes before History. Should he find out what Megan was doing? Should he apologize for freaking her out?

Megan was his only friend at school. If he didn't try to make things right with her, school could become a very lonely place.

Kyle headed towards the auditorium doors. Suddenly, they burst open and he saw Amber rush out, crying.

"Hey, what's wrong?" he asked.

Amber shook her head. "My costumes," she wailed. "All of my costumes are ripped apart!"

Chapter 8

BEHIND THE SCENES

Amber pushed past Kyle and ran down the hall. As Kyle turned to watch her go, Brendan walked up with a couple of friends.

"What did you do?" asked Brendan.

"Mind your own business," Kyle said.

"Did you make Amber cry?" Brendan demanded.

"You're mad," said Kyle. "I was just walking down here when she ran out of the theatre."

"Did you have a special rehearsal with J.B. or something?" asked Brendan. He moved closer to Kyle. Brendan's mates looked as big and angry as Brendan did.

"No," said Kyle.

"Then what are you doing here?" Brendan asked.

Kyle thought quickly. Should he tell Brendan he was following Megan inside? Would that make Megan look guilty?

Megan was hiding something. Would she actually go into the theatre dressing rooms and cut up Amber's costumes? Kyle didn't think she'd do it. But other people might believe she would.

"I'm only going to ask you one more time why you're here," Brendan said, frowning.

"I, uh, was going to meet Martian about my lines," said Kyle.

Brendan frowned. "Martian's at home, sick. Better come up with a better lie," he said.

"I saw Martian at lunch," said one of his friends.

Brendan spun around and yelled, "Stay out of this!"

The theatre door opened and J.B. entered the hall. She shot a glance at Brendan and his three friends. "Why aren't you boys in class? Have any of you seen Amber?" she asked.

One of Brendan's friends pointed down the hall. "She ran that way," he said.

J.B. walked up to Brendan. "You saved me from that light, so I'm going to give you some advice. Get to your lesson and forget about Kyle," she said.

Brendan stared at her for a moment. Then he looked down and walked away. His friends ran to catch up with him.

J.B. turned to Kyle. "I'm heading to the office," she said. "It seems we're dealing with more than just simple accidents. It's turned into vandalism. I believe Megan is looking for you inside."

"She is? Oh, thanks," said Kyle.

"One more thing," said J.B. "You know the school has rules about wearing hats inside the building. I'll take that." She held out her hand.

"Sorry," Kyle muttered. He was always forgetting about his hat. He wore it morning, noon, and night. It was easier to wear his hat sometimes than to worry about how his hair looked. He quickly pulled it off his head and handed it to the director. "Here," he said quietly.

"You'll get it back after the rehearsal," J.B. said.

Inside the theatre, Kyle saw that the work lights had been turned on above the stage. Megan was on the set, moving chairs around in the fake coffee shop.

Kyle walked onto the set. "Megan, need any help?" he asked.

Megan jumped and turned to look at him. "I didn't know you were there. You're always scaring me."

"I know," Kyle said. "I didn't mean to."

"You've got hair again," Megan said. "Spiky. What happened to your hat?"

"J.B. grabbed it," Kyle explained. "School rules, I guess."

"Did you hear about Amber's costumes?" asked Megan.

"Yes. I saw her run out of the theatre," said Kyle.

"This is getting serious," said Megan. "Scary, in fact."

"So does Amber get taken off your list of suspects?" Kyle asked.

Megan thought for a moment. "That's a good question," she said. "I don't know. If this were an Agatha Christie story, she would make Amber cut up her own costumes. No one would ever guess it would be her."

"Wow," said Kyle. "That's harsh."

"Anyway, can you help me move some chairs? I have an idea," said Megan. "About our so-called accident."

Megan and Kyle moved the chairs so that there was a clear path to the back of the coffee shop counter. Then Megan carried a chair over to the wall directly behind the counter. It was the wall section that had fallen the other night.

"Just make sure I don't kill myself," she told Kyle.

Megan climbed up on the chair and faced the wall section. She carefully examined the surface. Then she pulled a small torch out of her pocket and aimed it at the wall.

"Aha!" she cried.

"What?" said Kyle.

Megan pointed. Kyle saw a thin wire sticking out of the front of the wall. The wire was only a few inches long.

Megan handed Kyle the torch. She pulled out a pair of scissors from her other pocket and snipped off the wire. She stepped down off the chair. Then she handed the wire to Kyle.

Kyle looked at it. It was thin and clear. "Fishing line," he said.

Megan nodded. "And I think we'll find something even more interesting on the other side of the wall," she said.

They walked behind the set and found the back of the same wall section. The wall, like all the others, was made of a large wooden frame. Canvas was stretched across the frame and painted to look like a wall.

To give the frame more support, wooden strips crossed the back of the wall section. The extra wood also gave the wall extra weight. To keep the walls standing up, there were heavy metal weights on the bottom of the wall sections. Some wall sections were weighed down with small sandbags.

"Shouldn't we be getting to class?" asked Kyle.

"I thought you wanted to find out who's behind the accidents," said Megan.

She aimed her torch at the top of the wall. "See?" Megan said. "There it is." Another piece of wire was poking out of the wall on the backside. This piece was tied around one of the wooden strips.

"The tech guys did not put that there," said Megan. "This is how the wall fell over. Someone attached that fishing line to the wall. That was the first step. Then, all they had to do was pull it from the front to make it fall over."

"Or," said Kyle, "someone could have used it from behind. Those weights were moved off the bottom. The fishing line could have been used to keep the wall section in place. Then the crook lets go of the line. Bam! It falls forward."

"Yeah, it could have happened that way, too," said Megan.

"The line is so thin, no one would even see it," said Kyle.

Megan nodded. "It's invisible to the naked eye," she said.

"But who could have done this?" asked Kyle. "Everyone was on stage out front when the wall fell over. J.B. was talking to us, remember? I was there, Brendan, Amber, you, and everyone else. Anyone could be the criminal."

"This isn't as easy as Agatha Christie makes it seem," said Megan.

There was one person on Megan's list who hadn't been on the stage when the wall fell over. Martian. He'd been out in the auditorium, typing away on his laptop as usual.

"So he's in the clear," thought Kyle. "Isn't he?"

Chapter 9

THE KNIFE

That afternoon at rehearsal, no one was singing, no one was dancing, and definitely no one was having a good time.

Instead, the cast was scattered all over the auditorium. They were split into small groups. Everyone was whispering about the one person who should have been there, but wasn't.

J.B. stood up on the stage and clapped loudly to get everyone's attention. "We all know that Amber is not here today," she said

The cast got quiet.

"That does not, however, mean she won't be joining us in the future," J.B. said.

People started whispering again.

"It does mean that she is thinking things over," continued J.B. "But for now, we can't let that stop us. So tonight, Amber's lines will be read by Megan."

A few people cheered and clapped. Megan blushed.

"All right then," said J.B. "Let's do it. Act Three. Everyone on stage."

"Way to go, Megan!" said Kyle.

Megan had a funny smile on her face. Kyle figured she was probably nervous about having to stand on stage and read Amber's lines. Megan had always said she preferred working behind the scenes.

All the actors for Act Three started gathering on the stage. Megan picked up her script and ran down the center aisle of the theatre.

"Oof!" she cried. She tripped over Kyle's rucksack, which was lying in the aisle.

Everyone ran over to help. "Are you okay?" asked one of the other girls.

"Yeah, I'm okay," said Megan. "Just clumsy."

"Sorry about that," said Kyle. "That's my bag. I should have put it on a chair."

"No problem," said Megan. She glanced at the floor and frowned. "Oh, what's this? I must have knocked it out of your bag."

She reached down and picked up an object from the ground. Then she held it up in the light. It was a six-inch-long grey metal stanley knife. The blade stuck out at one end.

"That's not mine," said Kyle.

Some pieces of fabric were stuck on the end of the blade. Kyle frowned. The colours of the fabric looked familiar.

"That's the same material as Amber's costume in Act Two," cried one of Amber's friends. "I remember that green colour."

"He slashed Amber's costume," a girl yelled.

"What?" yelled Brendan. "How could you do that, Kyle?"

"It can't be the same material," said Kyle.

"Knives aren't allowed at school," said Martian calmly.

"It's not my knife," said Kyle.

"It came out of your bag," Martian said.

"There must be some mistake," said Kyle. "Someone must have put that there. I've never seen that knife before in my life."

J.B. quickly walked down the aisle. "Let me see that," she ordered.

"Calm down, people," said J.B. "Let me handle this." She took the knife from Megan and examined it closely. "Is that your bag, Kyle?" J.B. asked.

"Yeah," Kyle said slowly.

"Let's go to my office," J.B. said. She turned to the stage and said, "Everyone, keep rehearsing."

"Who'll do Kyle's lines?" asked Brendan.

"Hector," said J.B., pointing to a redheaded kid standing onstage. "You read them."

As Kyle walked past Megan, she kept her eyes on the floor. She wouldn't look at him.

J.B.'s office was a small room off the auditorium. Inside, Kyle sat down on the chair. "I can't believe this," he said. "I can't believe this is happening to me."

"What was that knife doing in your bag?" asked J.B.

"I don't know!" said Kyle. "I didn't put it there."

"I'm not accusing you," said J.B. "But the evidence is not good. The knife was in your

bag. You've been around when all the other accidents happened. You've been seen fighting with Brendan Foster. And on top of that, you're the new kid in town. People don't know you very well."

"So it's easy to blame me. Is that what you're saying?" asked Kyle.

"Yes. We need to find out who's responsible for the vandalism. Right now, you're the perfect target," said J.B. She paused. Then she said, "You're a good actor. A very talented actor. But that makes things more complicated. One thing about actors – it's harder to tell when they're lying."

"I'm not lying," said Kyle. "Give me a lie-detector test! Take my fingerprints!"

He thought about his conversation with Megan in the library. He'd told her that he had an evil mind, and that he was X the Unknown. Megan had been freaked out by how convincing he had sounded. He should never have told her that.

"People can fool lie detectors," said J.B. "And criminals sometimes wear gloves."

Kyle stared at her. He couldn't believe what had happened.

"I know, I know," said J.B. "I watch too much TV." She smiled, then walked over and opened the door. "Come on. We need to go to the office and report this," she said.

Kyle slowly stood up. He grabbed his rucksack. He scratched his head. That reminded him of something.

"Oh, do you still have my hat?" he asked. "Can I have it back?"

J.B. nodded. "It's on my desk," she said. She walked to her desk and looked down. Then she frowned. "Well, that's odd," she said. "Someone must have taken it. It's gone."

Chapter 10

WEIGHT OF EVIDENCE

Jake, the tech guy, came rushing into the director's office. "We found something else," he said.

Kyle and J.B. followed Jake back onto the stage. He led them behind the set to the back of the wall sections.

The place looked familiar to Kyle, but he was starting to get a funny feeling on the back of his neck. Something wasn't right.

"It's right over here," said Jake.

He led them to one of the wall sections. A group of tech guys and cast members were standing in a small circle. They stared at Kyle as he and J.B. walked over.

Will pointed to the bottom of the wall. "It's that," he said.

The wall was held up by two small wooden feet, just as the other wall sections were. But the section that Wendell pointed at did not have any weights holding the feet down. In fact, the bag of weights that was supposed to be holding it had been moved a couple of feet away.

"Just like the section that fell on top of Brendan," Kyle thought.

As Kyle stared at one of the weights on the stage floor, his heart grew cold. Under the heavy weight was a familiar object. His hat.

"I did not put that there!" Kyle said.

"This wall would have fallen over," said Will. "Just like the other one. Jake and I have been checking them since the last accident. We didn't want anyone to get hurt."

"Did you find this?" J.B. asked Will.

"No," said Will. He pointed to the group nearby. "Megan did," he said.

"Megan!" said Kyle. "I didn't do this."

"What were you doing backstage, Megan?" asked J.B.

"I was standing here by the coffee shop door," she explained. "I was waiting to make my entrance, like Amber does in Act Three."

"I didn't put that hat there," said Kyle. "I couldn't have!" He turned to J.B. "You know I couldn't have done this," Kyle went on. "You had my hat. You took it from me earlier today and had it in your office the whole time. Tell them I didn't do it."

J.B. frowned at Kyle. She said, "I don't know what you're talking about. I never had your hat in my office."

"Kyle!" exclaimed Megan.

"It was him," said Jake.

J.B. continued, "You must have dropped your hat when you were moving those weights."

"But I never did!" said Kyle. "You did take my hat! You said it was against the rules!"

"We need to go to the office right now, young man," said J.B. "Follow me."

Kyle felt like he had been dropped into another dimension. Was this really happening to him? It seemed as if he were trapped in a sci-fi film. Maybe this was a different Harrison Ford High School, and all of the students and teachers had been replaced by robots.

Kyle followed J.B. down the steps of the stage and towards the main doors. Everyone stared at him as he moved through the theatre.

"Where is Megan?" wondered Kyle. She was his only friend. She should be defending him. Why wasn't she walking next to him, trying to convince J.B. that the director was wrong?

"And why is J.B. lying?" he thought. That's what hurt Kyle the most. J.B. was sometimes hard to work with, but she was always fair. Was she the person who had been sabotaging the show? Why else would she be lying about Kyle's hat?

Kyle glanced quickly behind him and saw Megan talking to Martian on stage. They were whispering about something. About him? Megan and Martian had never been friendly towards each other before.

Kyle walked up the aisle behind J.B. He stepped over the spot where Megan had found the knife in his bag. "Technically," he thought, the knife was not really in my bag. Megan picked it up from the aisle."

Then Kyle had a terrible thought. "Did Megan bring the knife? Did she pretend to trip over my bag so she could pull the knife out of her pocket and say she found it?"

Megan was the person who had found his hat backstage, too. When Kyle thought about it, he realized that it would have been easy for Megan to slip into J.B.'s office and grab the hat. Backstage, in the dim shadows, it would have been easy for her to move the weights and shove his hat underneath. And no one would suspect Megan.

"Maybe that was why Megan couldn't look me in the face earlier," Kyle thought. "Because she was planning to betray me."

SETTING THE TRAP

In the hall outside the theatre, Kyle saw someone standing by the windows. A short, stocky guy in a black and gold letter jacket. Rick Thomas. "Why is he hanging around?" Kyle wondered. "Is Amber nearby?"

Kyle didn't have time to think about it. J.B. was walking briskly down the hallway. Kyle had to hurry to keep up with her.

Before they reached the office, J.B. quickly spun around. "All right, young man," she said. "Tell me what's going on."

"I told you, it wasn't me," said Kyle.

"I know it wasn't you," J.B. said. "How could it be? Your hat was in my office all day."

Kyle stared at her. "What?" he yelled. "Why did you lie about it?"

J.B. shook her head. "I'm sorry, Kyle," she said. "I just had to get you away from the stage. Someone in there is doing this. Do you have any idea who it is?"

Kyle said, "Megan and I made a list of suspects."

"You did?" asked J.B., folding her arms.

"Yeah. Megan thinks if we look for clues, we might be able to find out who's doing all this," said Kyle.

"Well, your silly hat was a good excuse for someone," said J.B. "Everyone knows you wear that hat. Anyone who walked into my office would have seen it."

Kyle thought about all the people who could have walked in and out of the director's office. Anyone connected with *Starcups!* could have. That didn't even include students from J.B.'s drama and speech classes who might have visited her during the day.

Then Kyle thought about Megan. He didn't know if he should mention his friend. He didn't want to get her in trouble without having real proof.

"Then . . . there's Megan," said J.B.

Kyle was stunned. "Can J.B. read my mind?" he wondered nervously.

"Uh, what do you mean?" asked Kyle.

"Megan. Megan Oliver," said J.B. "She's right there, behind you."

Kyle turned around. Megan was rushing down the hall towards them. "Wait, Kyle! Wait! Stop!" called Megan.

She ran up to J.B. and Kyle. "I tried texting you, Kyle," she said, gasping for breath. "Then I remembered that you always leave your mobile phone at home."

"What's going on?" demanded J.B.

"I think I know who's causing the accidents," Megan said. "And I think I know why." She smiled widely.

After a pause, Kyle finally said, "Who?"

"Oh, I don't have proof," said Megan. She looked at J.B. "I need Kyle to help me get the evidence. Can he help me, please?"

"This is serious," said J.B. "We're not talking about one of your mysteries."

"I think I know how to catch the vandal red-handed," said Megan. "And I can catch them tonight. But I'll need Kyle's help. As backup, you know."

"You don't think I'm X the Unknown?" asked Kyle.

"Not anymore," said Megan. "I mean, not like I ever did. But, um, now I'm sure. I saw something backstage that convinced me."

"You saw who put my hat under the weight?" said Kyle.

Megan shook her head. "Nope," she said. "But I saw someone put something else on the set. Something that doesn't belong there."

"Megan, you need to tell me what's going on," said J.B.

"But then I still won't have proof," Megan protested. "I mean, you won't have proof either. It will be my word against theirs. That's another reason I need Kyle. As a witness."

Kyle looked at J.B. She frowned and said, "As long as what you're planning isn't illegal. Or dangerous."

"I swear on my goldfish's grave," said Megan.

J.B. gazed at her. "I have a bad feeling about this," she said. "But go ahead."

Megan and Kyle ran down the hall. Megan explained her plan.

First, they had to get Kyle into J.B.'s office without anyone from the cast or crew seeing him. Megan said they needed everyone to think that Kyle was the crook, and that he was going to be thrown out of the show.

Megan explained, "That will give the real crook a false sense of security. Then they'll think that they're off the hook."

Once Kyle was in J.B.'s office, Megan went back into the theatre.

"Kyle Sutton has confessed to being the person behind all the accidents," Megan said.

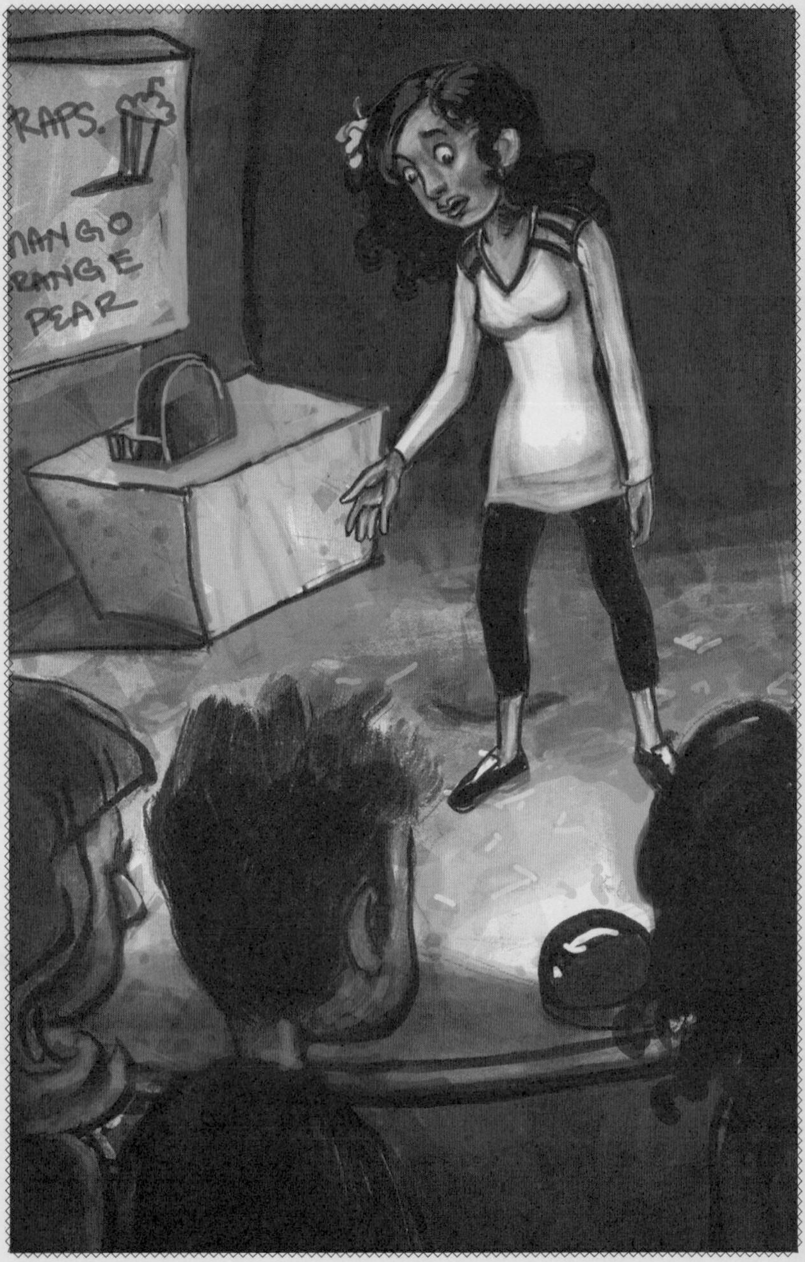
RAPS.
MANGO
RANGE
PEAR

Cast members gasped. "I knew it!" said Brendan.

"Tomorrow morning, J.B. and I will examine the set," Megan went on. "We're sure that Kyle left some evidence behind, and we are going to find it. We will check every costume, every wall section, and every prop used in the show. But for now, J.B. told me to say that rehearsal is over for the night. So go home, work on your lines, and be ready for practice tomorrow. Thank you."

The theatre emptied quickly. As soon as the doors shut and the last sounds of conversation died away, Megan ran to the theatre office. She stuck her head inside the door and whispered, "Kyle! Are you ready?"

Kyle had been sitting on the couch. "No," he said, getting to his feet. "But I guess we'll do this anyway."

Chapter 12

SCISSORS

All the lights were off in the theatre. Only the faint red glow of the exit signs burned in the darkness.

Megan and Kyle carefully made their way backstage. Megan aimed the thin beam from her torch on the floor ahead of them.

Neither of them spoke. Slowly, they walked behind the *Starcups!* set. They came to the wall section where Kyle's hat had been found. The weights had been put back onto the feet of the wall.

"My hat's gone," Kyle said.

"Don't worry about it," whispered Megan. "I put it in my rucksack. And keep your voice down. We don't want to scare anyone away."

"Who?" said Kyle. "Who would we be scaring away?"

"Sssssh!" said Megan, turning off her torch. "I think I can hear something."

The two of them quickly stepped behind one of the tall black curtains that hung backstage. The curtains were used to hide the backstage wall from the audience whenever a door was opened on the set. Now, the curtain was the perfect hiding place in the shadowy gloom of the empty set.

"I hear it too," whispered Kyle.

Soft footsteps were moving across the wooden stage. Someone was walking towards the walls of the set.

Then the footsteps stopped. Slowly, the door in the coffee shop opened. Kyle could see a person standing in the doorway. The reddish glow from the exit signs was just enough to show a dark outline. Kyle couldn't tell who it was. He couldn't even tell if the person was male or female.

"Who is that?" Kyle whispered.

"Just watch," Megan whispered back.

The person used the faint glow from the digital screen of a mobile phone to light the way behind the set. Carefully, the person stepped behind the wall. Kyle could see the person's hand moving along the wall. The person was searching for something.

Just as the person's other hand reached up, Megan stepped out from behind the curtain. She aimed her torch at the person's startled face.

"Martian!" she said.

"Who are you supposed to be?" said
Martian. "Inspector Morse?"

"What's that in your hand?" asked Kyle.

"Great," Martian said calmly. "The whole
cast is here." He stared at Kyle. "I thought
you were kicked out," Martian went on. "You
know, Megan, you could get jail time for
helping a criminal."

"Just tell us what you're doing here,"
Kyle demanded.

"Planning another little accident?"
Megan asked.

"Preventing another accident," said
Martian. He held up his hand. Megan shone
her light on it. A small electronic gadget lay in
Martian's palm.

"A recorder?" asked Kyle.

Martian nodded. "A voice-activated recorder. It only turns on if someone starts talking," he explained.

"What were you planning to do with that?" asked Megan.

"The same thing you're trying to do," said Martian. "Catch the crook. I put one of these on the wall that fell over. It got damaged in the fall, so I decided to try again."

Megan turned to Kyle. "I saw Martian checking that recorder after you and J.B. left," she said. "I assumed he was the vandal. That's why I wanted you to come here tonight and help me catch him."

"When you told the cast you were going to look for evidence, I thought I'd better come back and remove this," Martian explained. "I was worried that you might think it was a trap or something like that."

"You were hoping to record evidence with it?" asked Kyle.

"Yes. I thought it might give me a clue to who was behind these accidents," said Martian. "I put the first recorder on the set to help me hear lines better. I can't catch every mistake during a rehearsal. I planned to listen to the recorder at night and then make notes. But when the accidents started happening, I thought it could be used for something else. Getting evidence."

"Did you get any?" asked Megan.

"Uh, no, not so far," said Martian.

"Well, we did," said Kyle. He led them to the wall section that had toppled over on to Brendan. "Look up there," he said. Megan shone her tiny torch where Kyle pointed. The short piece of fishing line was still tied to the wooden strip.

"It sticks out on the other side, too," said Kyle. "But just an inch or so."

"Clever," said Martian. "That's pretty high up. How did the person use it to knock over the wall?"

"We're not exactly sure," said Megan.

Kyle heard a noise and froze. "Turn off that light," he whispered. They could hear another set of footsteps out in the theatre. Kyle, Megan, and Martian hid behind one of the black curtains.

The footsteps walked across the stage. The steps approached the back wall of the coffee shop set. But the coffee shop door did not open.

"They're right on the other side," whispered Megan.

Feet shuffled on the other side of the wall. Then Kyle heard a swishing sound. "A pair of scissors?"

"Someone's cutting off that fishing line," thought Kyle. "They want to get rid of the evidence."

There was another sound Kyle was waiting to hear. He didn't hear it.

"That's it," Kyle told himself. "Now I know who did it."

He had the final clue. A sound that never came.

"Push it over," whispered Kyle.

"What?" said Martian. "Are you kidding?"

"Just do it," said Kyle. "Push it. Now!"

The three students rushed out from behind the black curtain. In the darkness, they pushed against the wall. Their combined weight was enough to push it over.

CRASH!

Chapter 13

X THE UNKNOWN

A groan came from the other side of the wall.

"Come on!" yelled Kyle. He ran through the open coffee shop door. In the red glow of the exit signs, he made his way to the fallen wall.

"Megan!" he shouted. "Turn on your torch!"

"I can do better than that!" Megan called from far away.

Harsh white lights snapped on overhead. Mindy had run over to the backstage wall and found the switch for the work lights.

Martian and Kyle lifted up the fallen wall section. There was the crook, sprawled on the floor.

Kyle was not surprised by who he saw. He walked closer. "Trying to get rid of the evidence?" he asked.

The tall, blonde-haired boy on the floor glared at Kyle.

"You've been a pain ever since you got here, Kyle," Brendan said.

Megan rushed on to the set. "Brendan, how could you?" she cried.

Martian snapped a few photos of Brendan with his phone. "I think J.B. will be interested in seeing these," he said.

"You're the lead in the show," said Kyle. "What's the big idea?"

"You're the big idea, funny guy," said Brendan, rubbing an egg-sized bump on his head. "Don't tell me you weren't trying to ruin my lines. Wreck my part. Take all the laughs."

"Now it makes sense," said Martian, turning to Kyle. "He was trying to get you in trouble. With you out of the show, he wouldn't have to compete with you onstage."

"Did you know it was him?" Martian asked Kyle.

Kyle shook his head. "Not until we heard his scissors cut that fishing line," he said. "I knew it had to be the crook getting rid of the evidence. But I didn't know for sure that it was Brendan until I noticed that something was missing. Then I was absolutely positive that it was him."

"What was missing?" asked Megan.

"Another sound," said Kyle. "A chair being moved over in front of the wall."

"How did you know there should be a chair?" Martian asked.

Kyle smiled. "Remember when you found that string in the first place, Megan? You had to use a chair to see it. It's so far off the ground, only one person in the show would be able to cut it without using a chair. The tallest person in the show. Brendan."

"This will definitely be going on my blog," said Martian.

"I figured Brendan pulled the wall over on himself using that fishing line," Kyle explained. "When he was underneath it, in that space by the counter, he just snapped the line. He was trying to break it off. But a few inches got stuck in the wall."

"I'm calling J.B. right now," said Megan. She pulled her mobile phone out of her pocket.

"She can't kick me out of the show," complained Brendan. "I'm the star. No one's as good as me. Who else would she get to do it?"

Kyle rolled his eyes.

"Hi, J.B.," said Megan into her phone. "I'm staring at your new lead for the musical. His name is Kyle Sutton."

About the Author

Michael Dahl is the author of more than 100 books for children and young adults. He has twice won the AEP Distinguished Achievement Award for his nonfiction. His Finnegan Zwake mystery series was chosen by the Agatha Awards as one of the five best mystery books for children in 2002 and 2003. He collects books on poison and graveyards, and lives in a haunted house.

About the Illustrator

Tiffany Prothero is a freelance illustrator. Along with illustrating for magazines and books, she enjoys taking care of her feral cats and spending time with her partner, Mark.

Glossary

auditorium large room where people gather for events like plays

backstage area behind the stage

criminal someone who commits a crime

director person in charge of putting on a play

evidence information and facts that help prove something

memorize learn something by heart

motives reasons for doing something

rehearsal practise for a play

script written text of a play

suspects people who may be responsible for a crime

vandalism act of damaging someone else's property

MORE ABOUT THE QUEEN OF CRIME

Agatha Christie, the Queen of Crime, is the most famous mystery writer in the world. She has also sold more books than any other writer. Her 80 mysteries have been translated into at least 103 languages and sold more than 4 billion copies!

Her mystery play *The Mousetrap* has been playing in London non-stop since 1952. It has already had more than 20,000 performances. In fact, it still holds the record for the world's longest-running play.

Two of Agatha Christie's most famous detectives were Miss Jane Marple and Hercule Poirot. Miss Marple was an elderly English woman who lived in a small town. Hercule Poirot was a private detective from Belgium who lived in London.

In the 1940s, Agatha Christie wrote the last two books that featured her detectives. Then she had the books sealed in a bank vault.

The books were not published until after her death on 12 January 1976.

Agatha Christie's books are famous for their clever, twisting plots. Readers could never solve the mystery until the very last page.

Often, the villain in her stories was the least likely suspect – the person who seemed undoubtably innocent. Christie was a master at tricking her readers, even though she always gave all the clues.

One of her famous stories, called *And Then There Were None*, is about a group of ten people trapped on an isolated island. One by one they are killed, each in a different manner, until no one is left alive. And the killer? Well, it's not the last person who dies!

How does Agatha Christie do it? She's the Queen.

Discussion Questions

1. Why was Brendan causing trouble in the musical?

2. Kyle joined the musical's cast so that he could make friends. What are some other ways for a new person at a school to make friends?

3. While you read this book, did you know that Brendan was the criminal? Did you ever think that the criminal could be someone else? If so, who, and why?

Writing Prompts

1. Have you ever been in a play? Write about it. If you haven't been in one, would you like to? Why or why not?

2. Do you know any other books, TV programmes, or films about plays and musicals? Write about how this book is different from other stories about plays and musicals.

3. Sometimes it's interesting to think about a story from another person's point of view. Try writing chapter 12 from Brendan's point of view. What does he see and hear? What does he think about? How does he feel?

Other books in the series